The Three Little Pigs

Illustrated by Dorothea King

Brimax Books · Newmarket · England

Once upon a time there were
three little pigs.
One day, their mother said,
"You are old enough to look after
yourselves now. It is time for
you to go out into the world
and build homes of your own."
The three little pigs were
very excited.
"Goodbye," they called as they
set off along different paths.

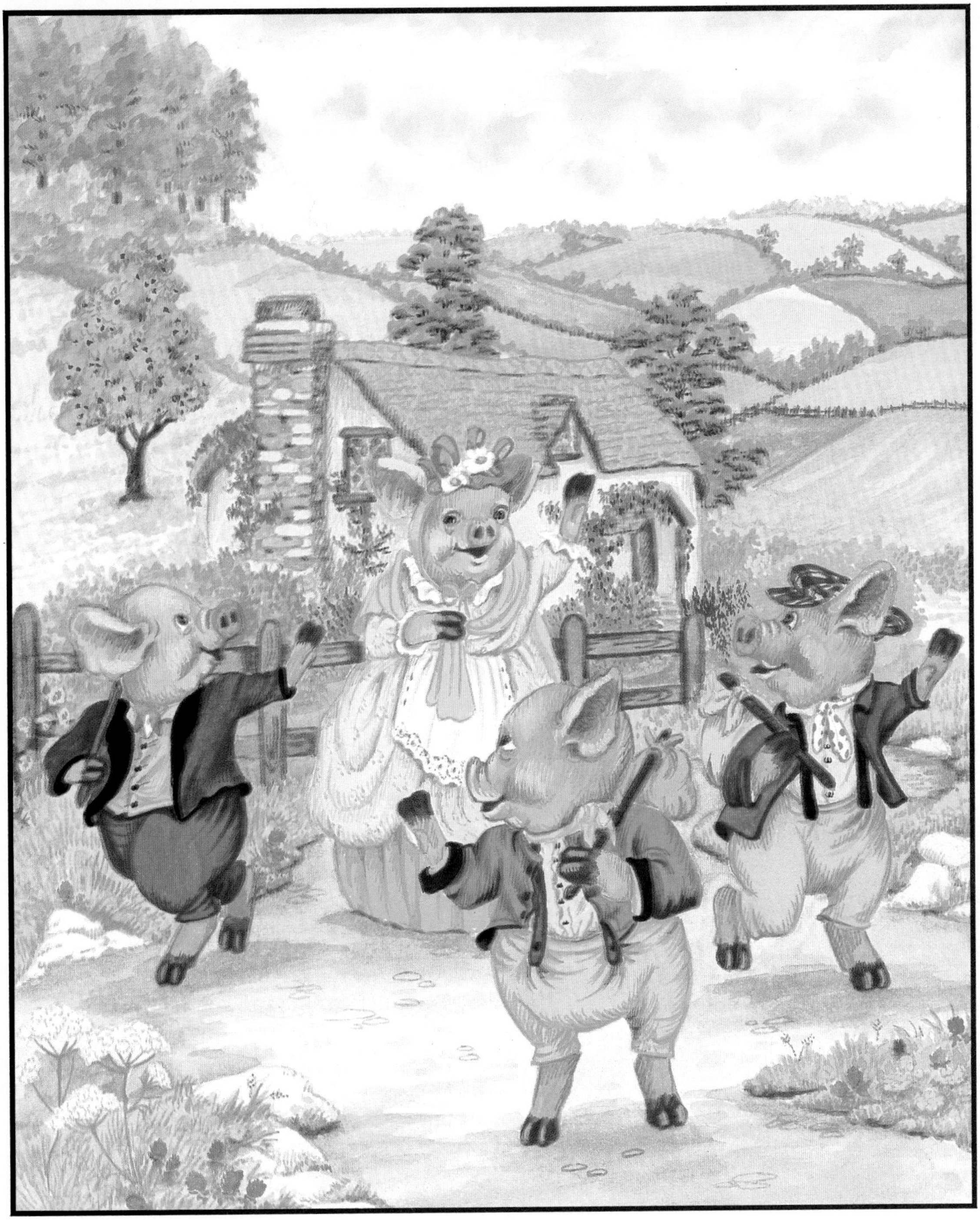

The first little pig always did
things in a hurry. He built
a house of straw. It was
not very strong.
One day a wicked old wolf
came to the door. The wolf
knocked at the door and called,
"Open the door little pig and let
me come in." He wanted the little
pig for his dinner.

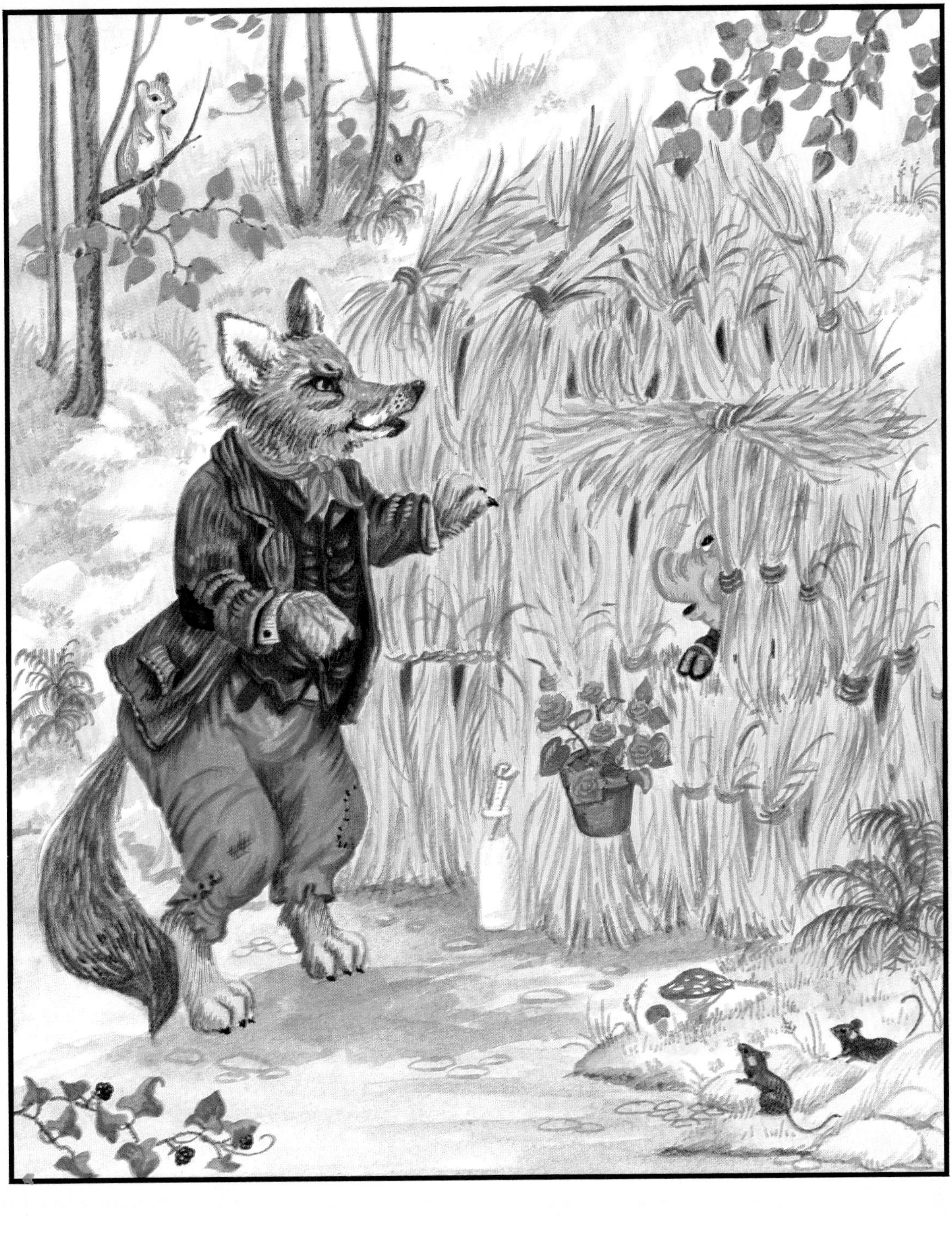

The first little pig
shivered and shook.
''By the hair on my chinny
chin chin, I will not open
the door and let you come in.''
''Then I will huff and I will puff
and blow your house down,''
growled the wolf.
And he huffed and he puffed
until the house of straw
blew away. And that was
the end of the first little pig.

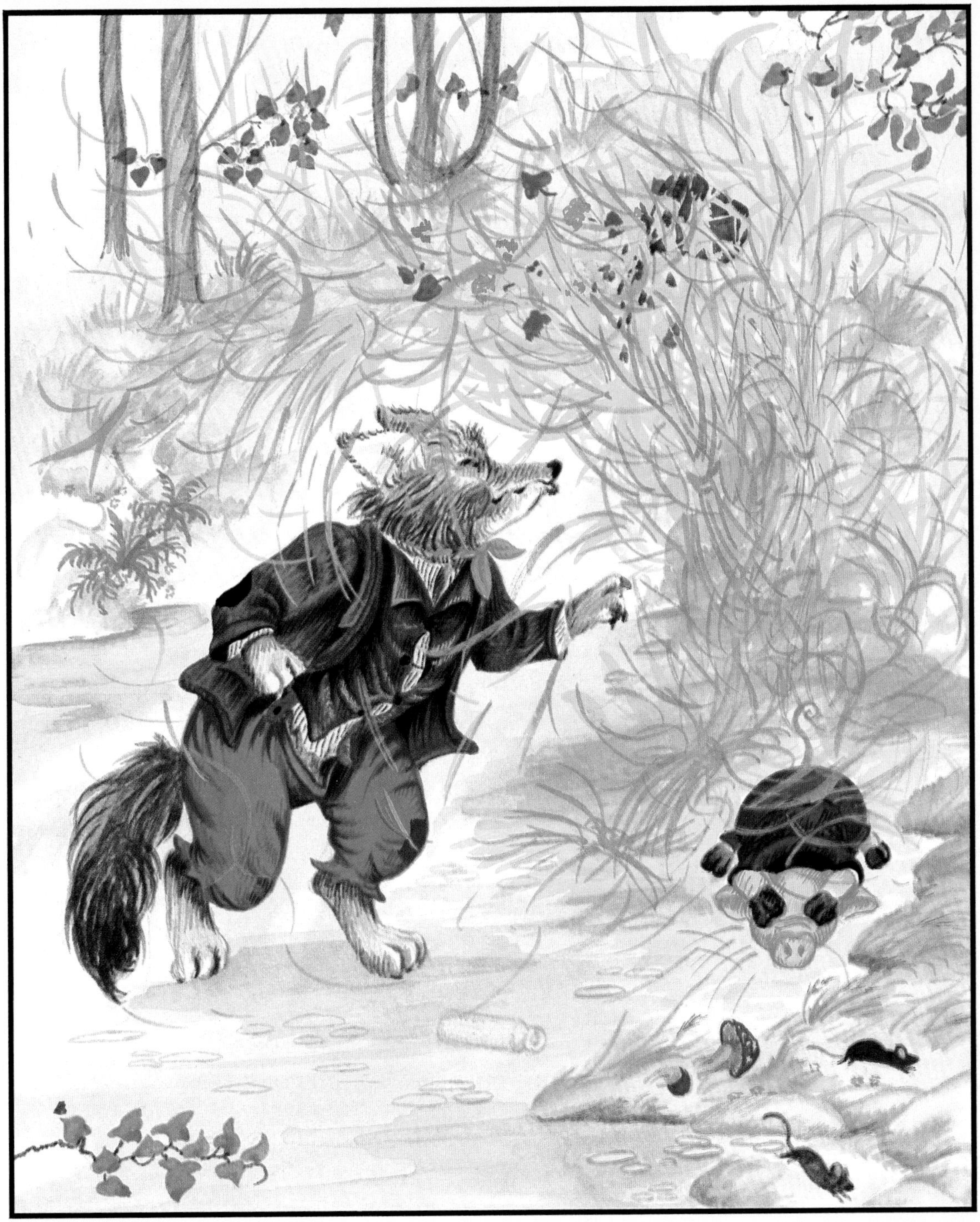

The second little pig never
finished a job. He built
a house of sticks. It was
full of gaps and not very strong.
One day the wicked old wolf
came to the door. The wolf
knocked at the door and called,
"Open the door little pig
and let me come in." He wanted
the little pig for his dinner.

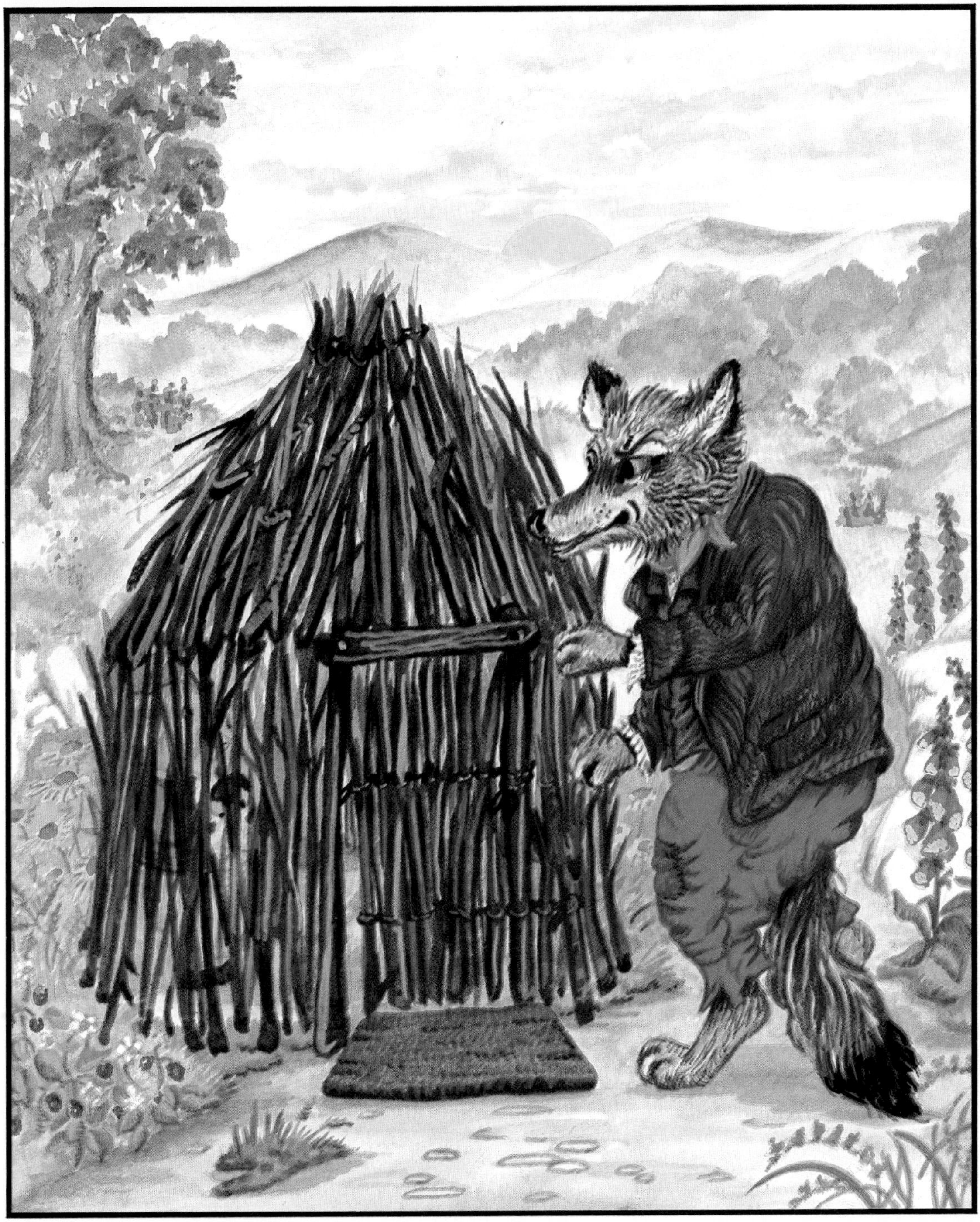

The second little pig
shivered and shook.
"By the hair on my chinny
chin chin, I will not open
the door and let you come in."
"Then I will huff and I will puff
and blow your house down,"
growled the wolf.
And he huffed and he puffed
until the house of sticks fell
down. And that was the end
of the second little pig.

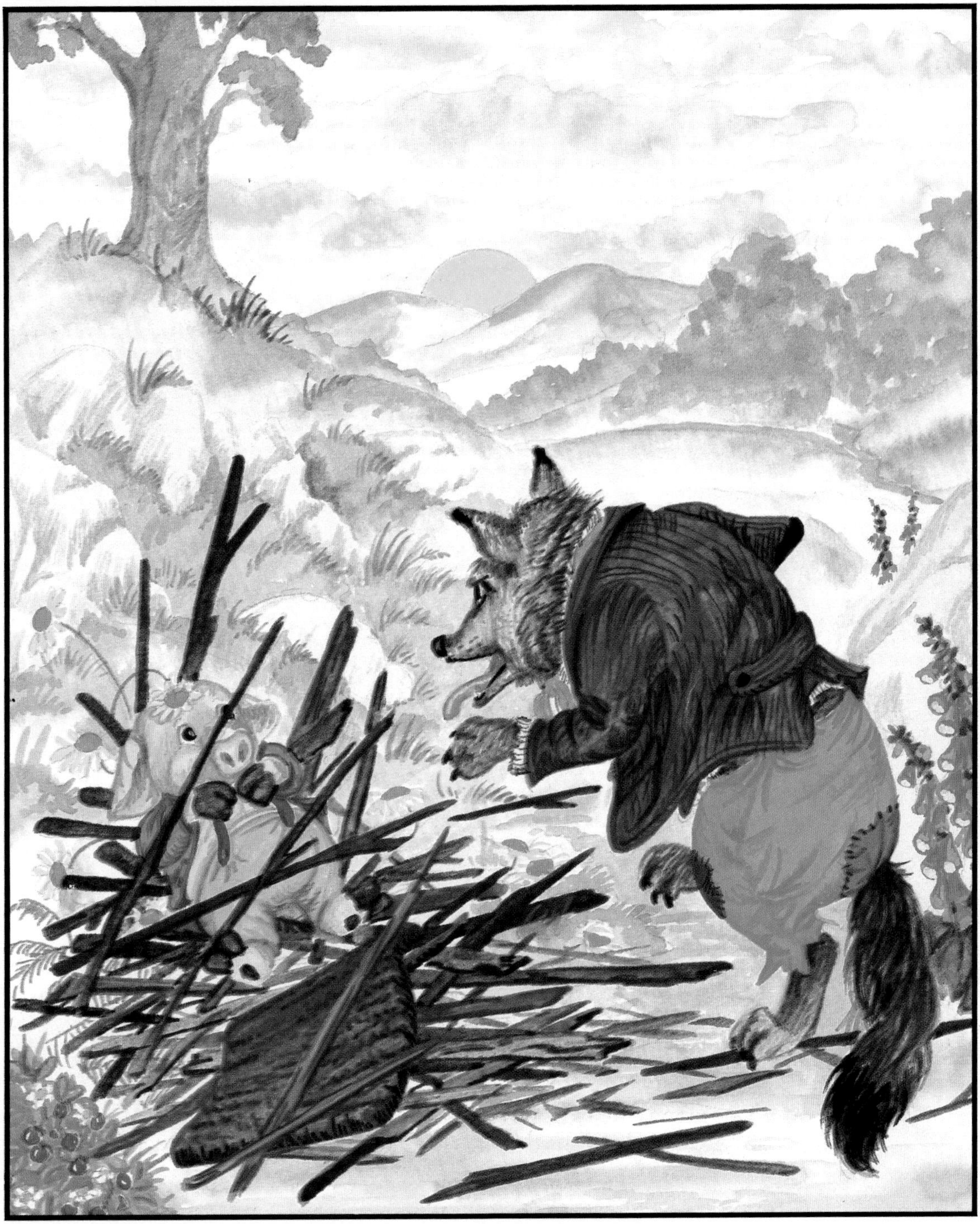

The third little pig always did
things properly. He built a house
of bricks. It was snug and warm
and very strong. One day the
wicked old wolf knocked at
the door and called,
"Open the door little pig
and let me come in." He wanted
the little pig for his dinner.

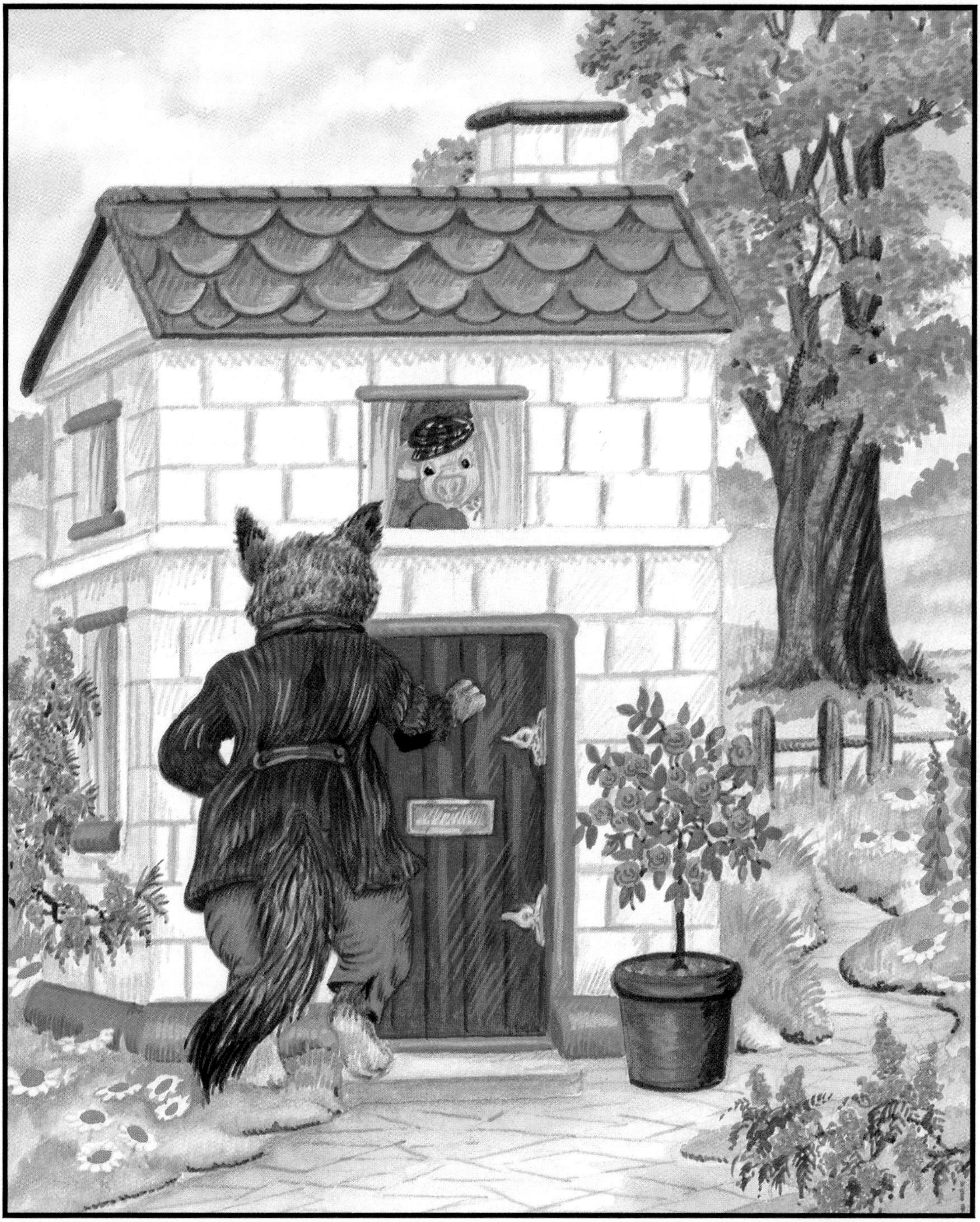

The third little pig
shivered and shook.
"By the hair on my chinny
chin chin, I will not open
the door and let you come in."
"Then I will huff and I will puff
and blow your house down,"
growled the wolf.

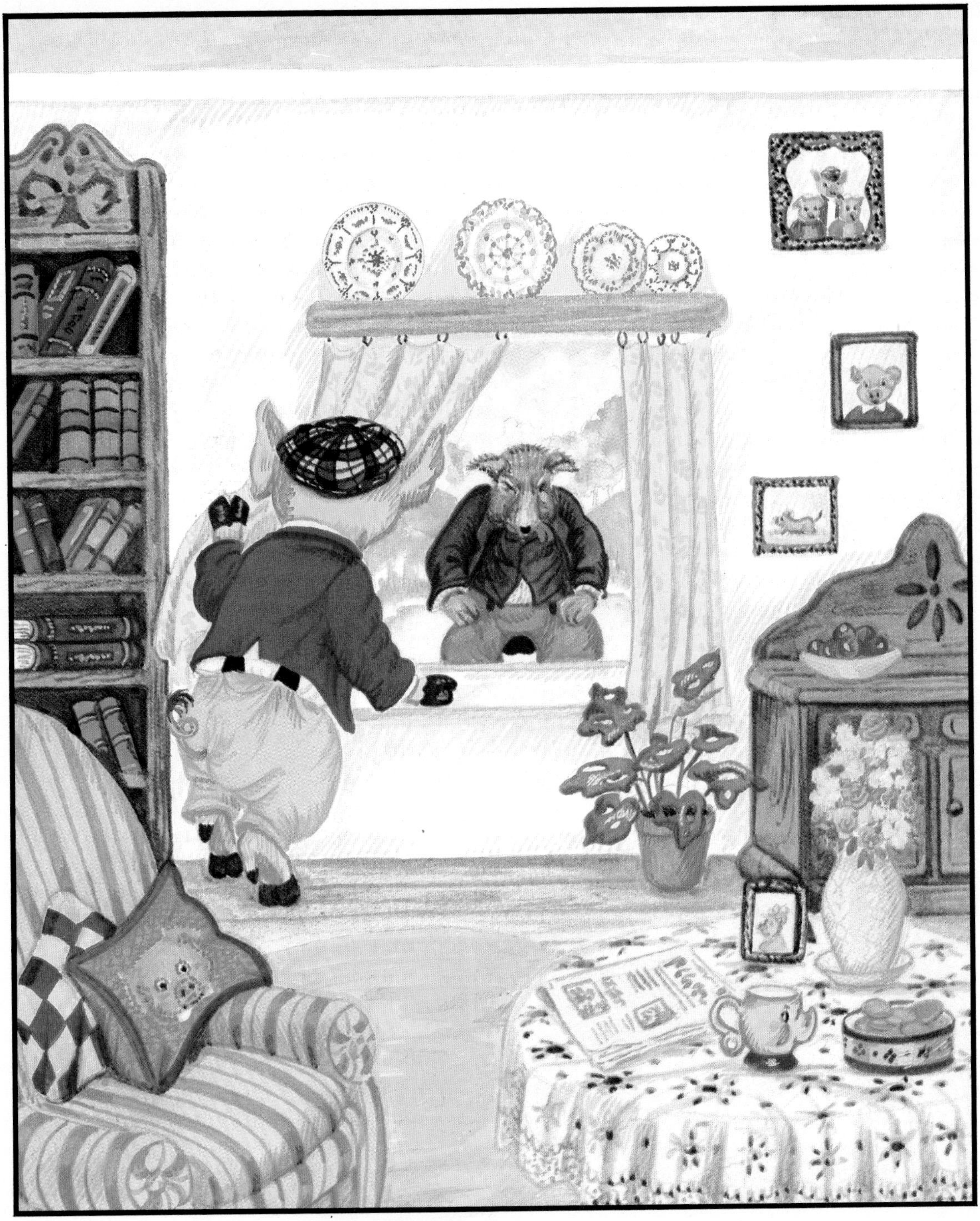

The wolf huffed and puffed until he was out of breath. The house of bricks stood firm.
He could not blow it down.
He would have to catch the little pig out of the house.
"Little pig," he called, "Meet me at the orchard at ten o'clock tomorrow morning. I will show you where the best apples are."

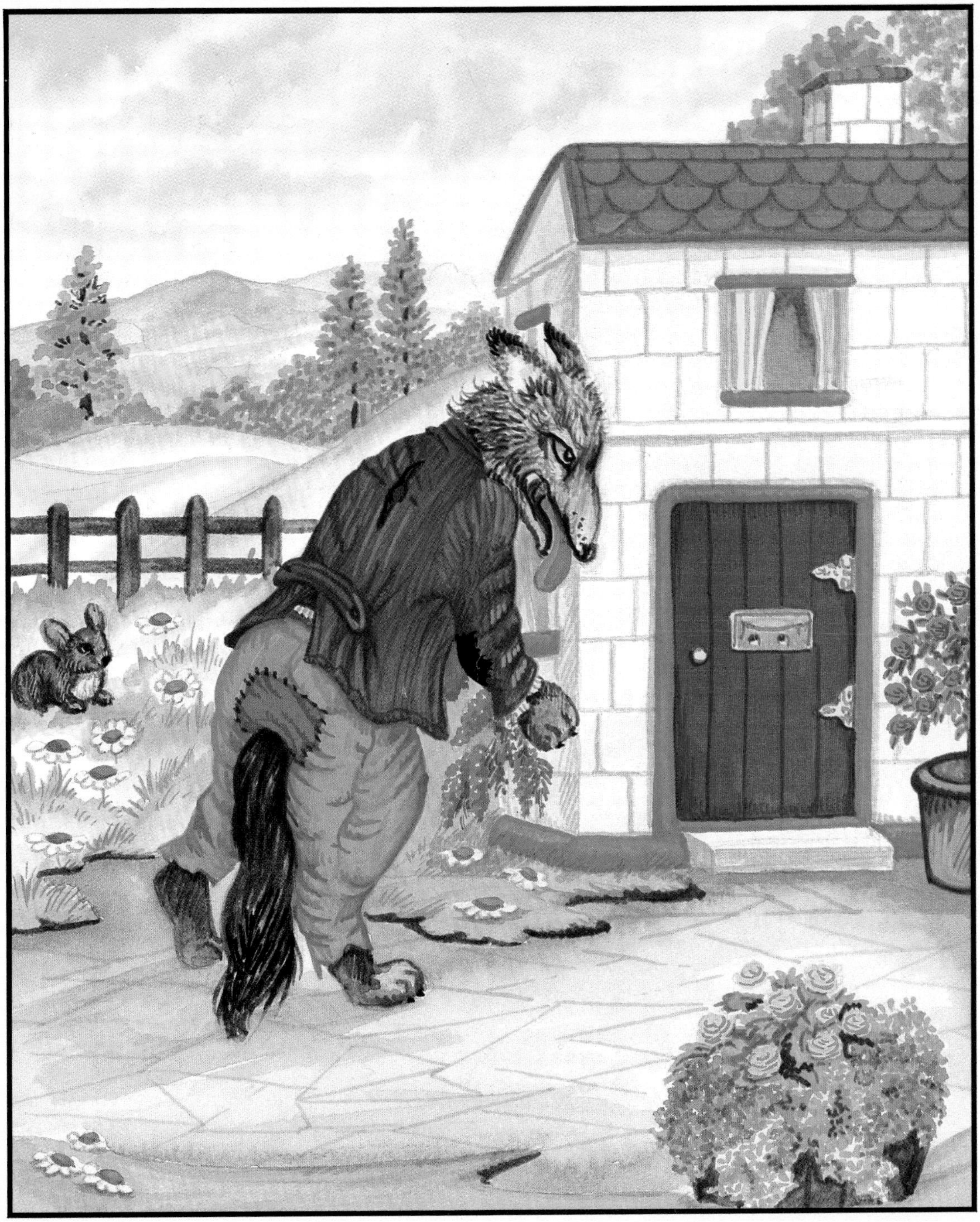

The third little pig knew the
wolf was trying to trick him.
He got up early the next morning.
He went to the orchard
and picked the best apples.
He was safely home by ten o'clock.
When the wolf got to the orchard
and found the best apples were
gone he was very angry.

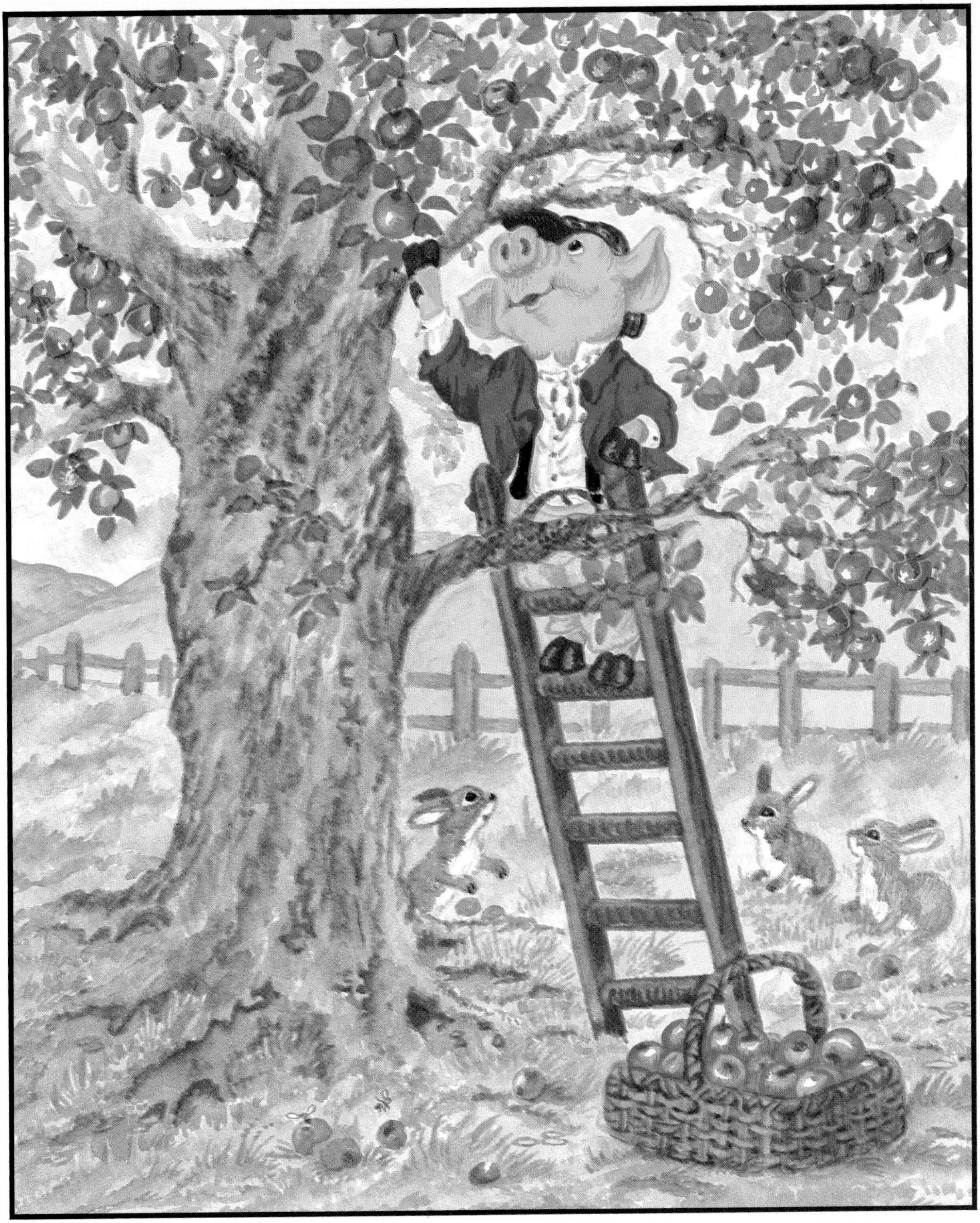

The wolf went back to the house.
"Are you going to market
tomorrow?" he called.
"Yes," said the little pig.
"Then I will meet you at eight
o'clock. We can go together."
said the wolf.
The little pig got up very early
the next morning.
"I will be home before the wolf
is awake," said the little pig.
But the wolf got up early too.

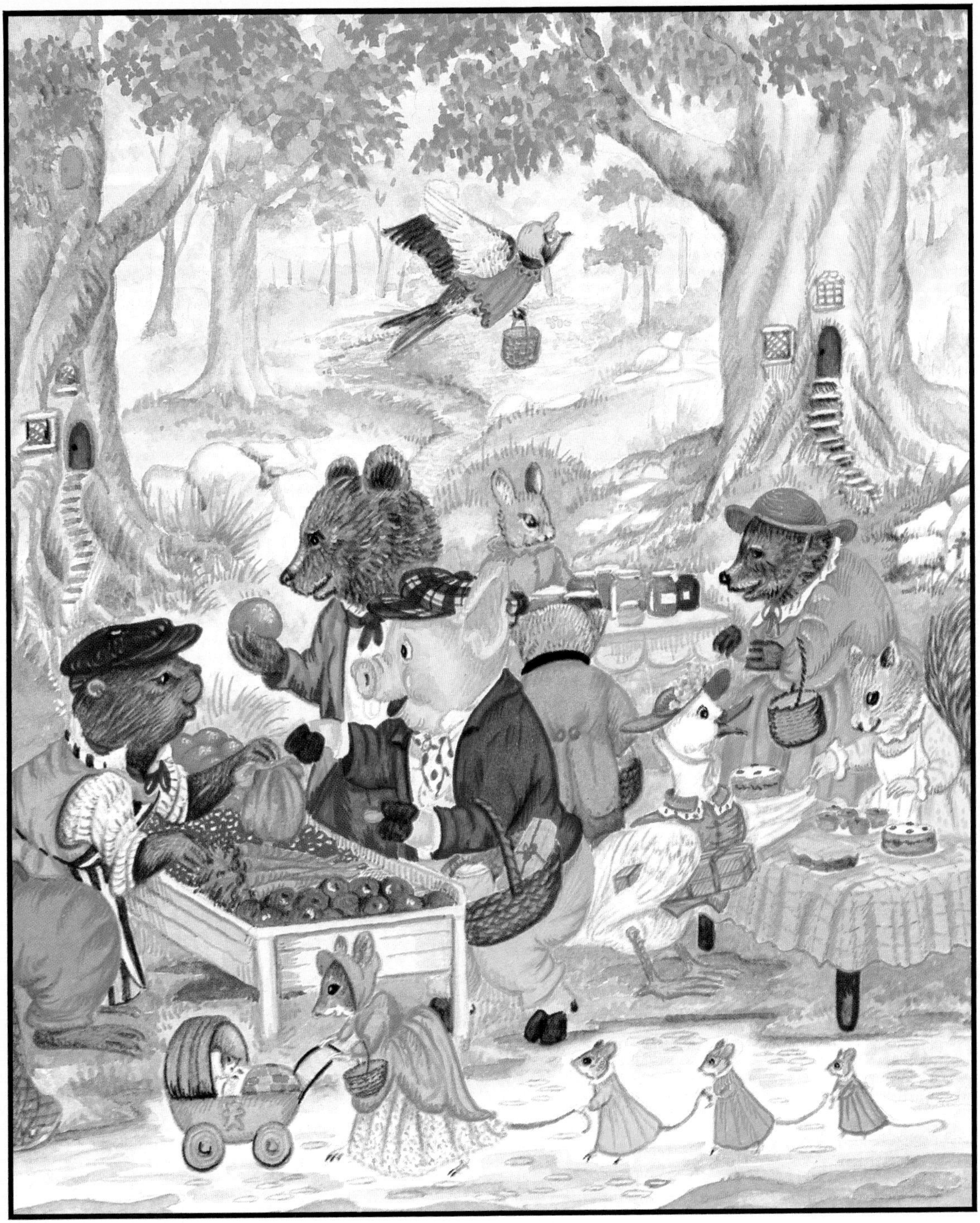

As the little pig walked home
he saw the wolf coming up
the hill. The little pig hid
in an empty milk churn.
The churn began to roll down
the hill. Faster and faster.
It ran the wolf down. He could
not believe his eyes when
he saw the little pig hop from
the milk churn, run into the
house and slam the door.

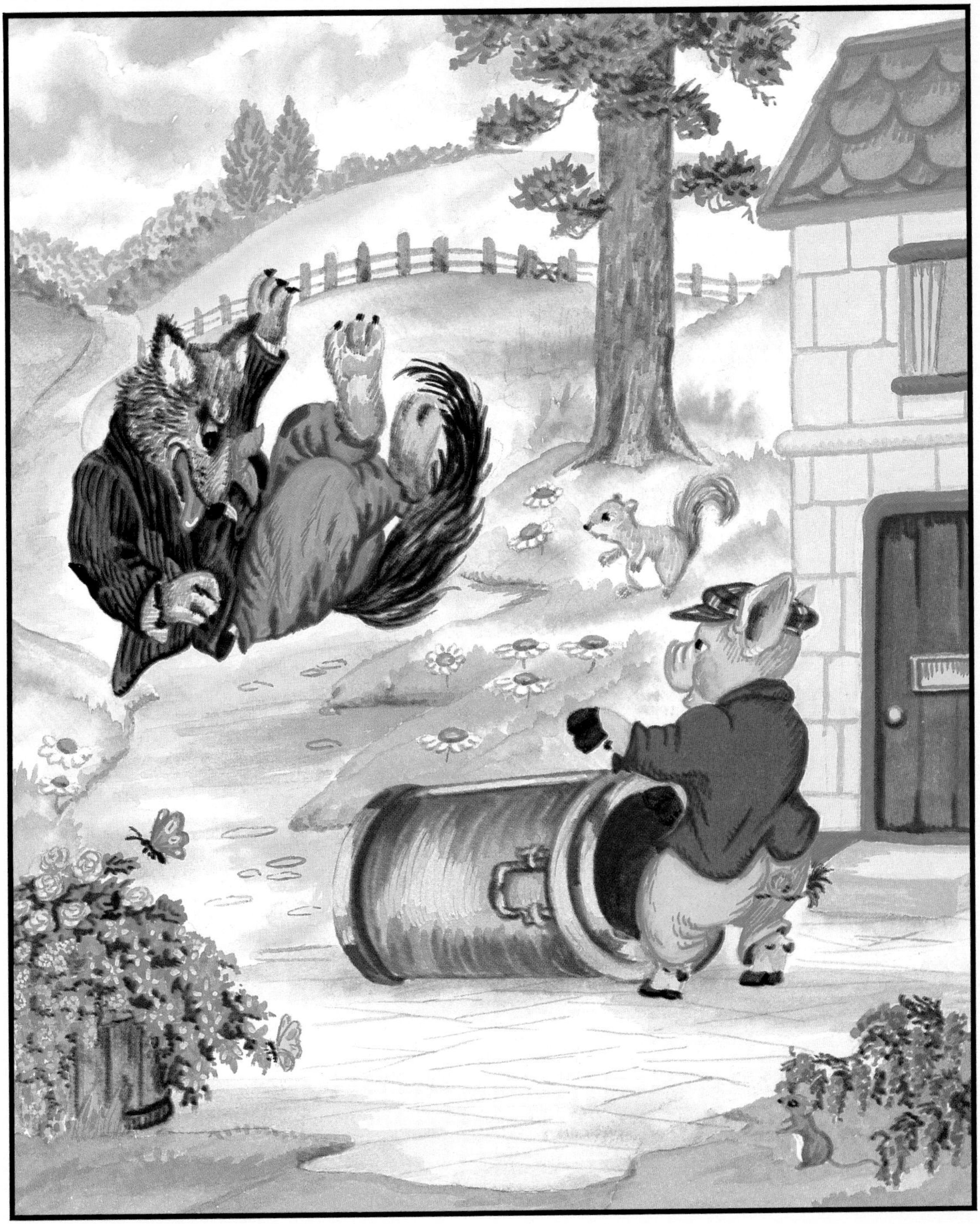

By now the wolf was really angry.
If he could not catch the little
pig outside the house, then he
would have to get inside.
He would have to go down
the chimney.
The third little pig heard the wolf
scrambling about on the roof.

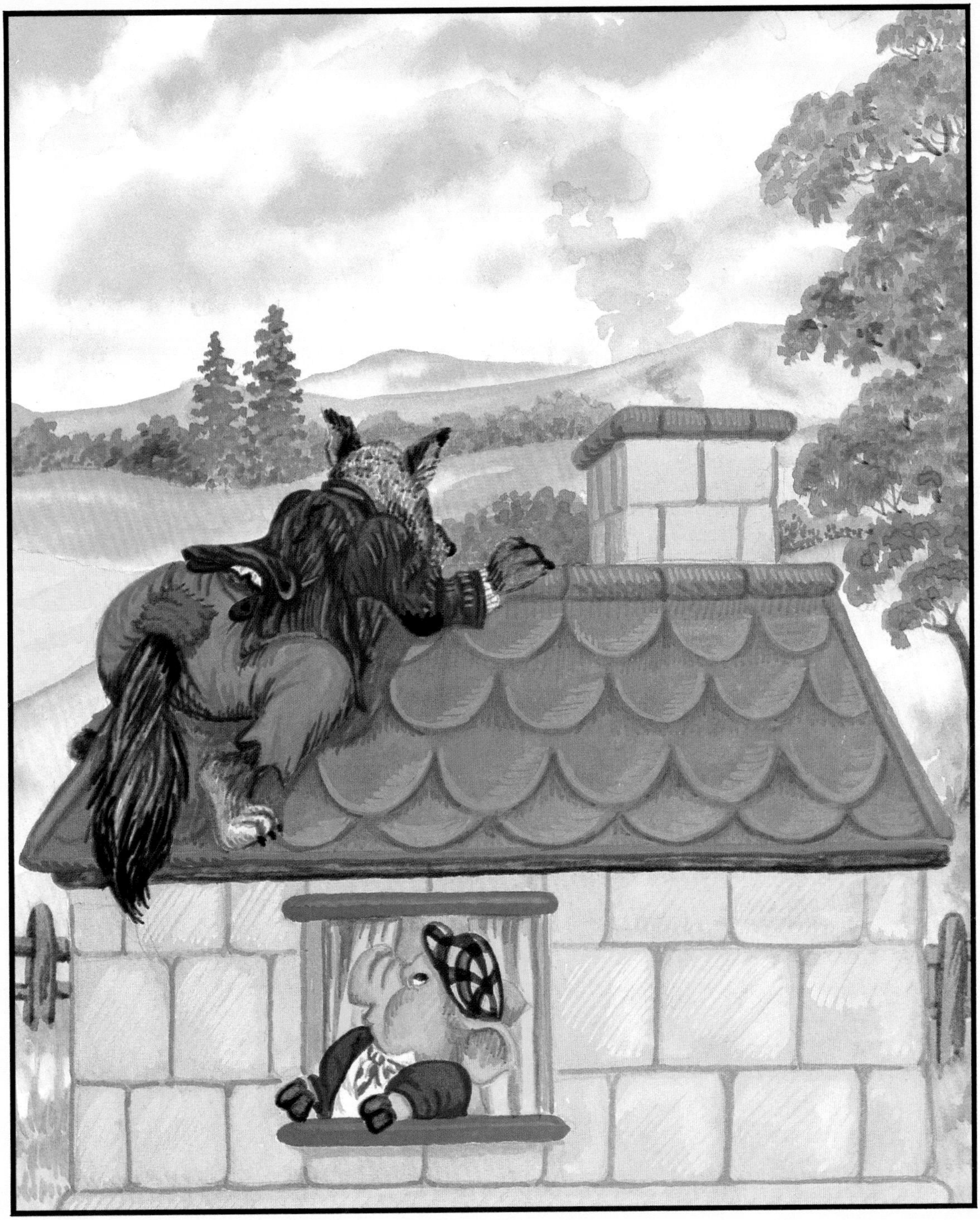

"The wicked wolf will never catch
me," cried the little pig. He put
a pot full of water on the fire
and waited. There was a rumbling
in the chimney. Suddenly there
was a great splash! The wicked
old wolf had fallen into the pot.
That was the end of him.
And the third little pig
lived happily ever after.

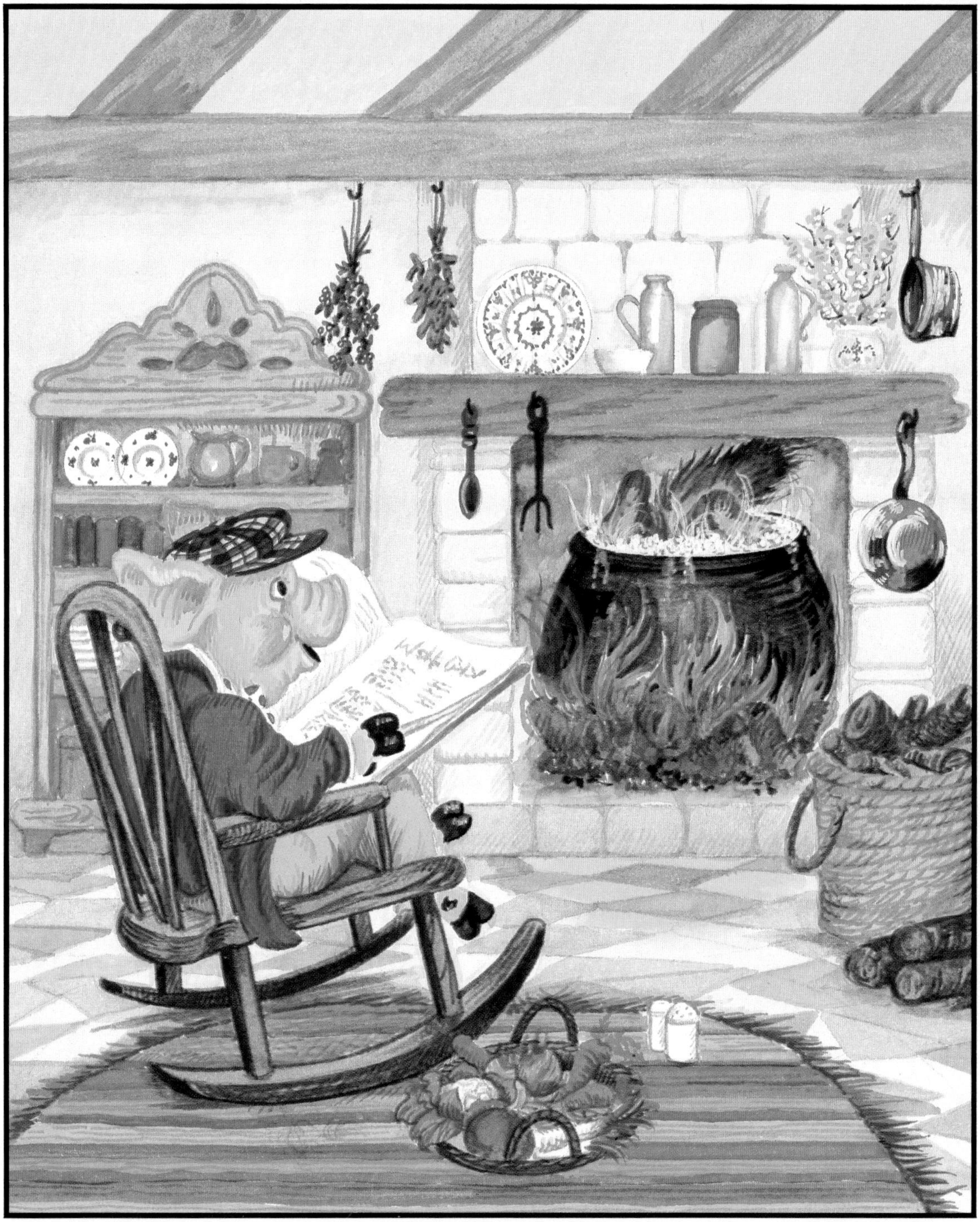